The adventures c

Mr. Fuzzy Ears

Searching for a furry friend

To my husband, Gary, who is crazier about dogs than I am!

To my mom, Betty Shaffer, who brings books to life with her readings.

To my friend, Kitty, and all Humane Societies.

And to our Scamp — "Mr. Fuzzy Ears" — my inspiration
for this book and for how to live life.

Mr. Fuzzy Ears lived with his human mom and
dad and he loved them very much.

And they loved him, too!

But as happy as Mr. Fuzzy Ears was, he was still
sad because he wanted a furry friend to play with.

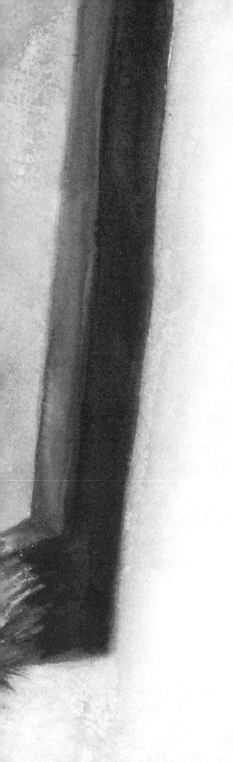

Even as a baby, he searched for a friend to play with.

He asked the puppy in the mirror, but the puppy just stared back.

So Mr. Fuzzy Ears began to search...

He knew there was a mouse scurrying around in the cupboard and Mr. Fuzzy Ears tried to find him.

Mr. Fuzzy Ears said,

"Hi! Would you like to come play with me?"

The mouse said, "Mr. Fuzzy Ears, I'd like to play with you, but I'm shy and won't leave my cupboard. Why don't you come in?"

But when Mr. Fuzzy Ears tried to squeeze into
Mr. Mouse's cupboard, he got stuck.

"Help, Mom!   I can't get out!"

So Mom came running and
pulled out the cupboard drawer.

"Whew! Thanks, Mom!" Mr. Fuzzy Ears said.

"Thanks anyway, Mr. Mouse, but I think
I need to look somewhere else."

"Maybe I should look outside," thought Mr. Fuzzy Ears.

He knew a family of chipmunks lived nearby.
So he searched and found them in the hedge.

"Would you come
play with me?" he asked.

But Mrs. Chipmunk said, "We are shy and won't leave
our nest. And you're too big to play here. So go away!"

"I'm sorry," Mr. Fuzzy Ears said, and he sadly walked away.

Then Mr. Fuzzy Ears saw Mr. Squirrel in the tree. "Would you come play with me?" he asked.

But Mr. Squirrel just sniffed and dropped an acorn on Mr. Fuzzy Ears' head.

"Ouch!"

"Oops, sorry!" said Mr. Squirrel.
"Maybe you can come play when
  you learn to climb my tree?"

Mr. Fuzzy Ears said, "No thanks."
His head hurt too much.

This was not a very good day.

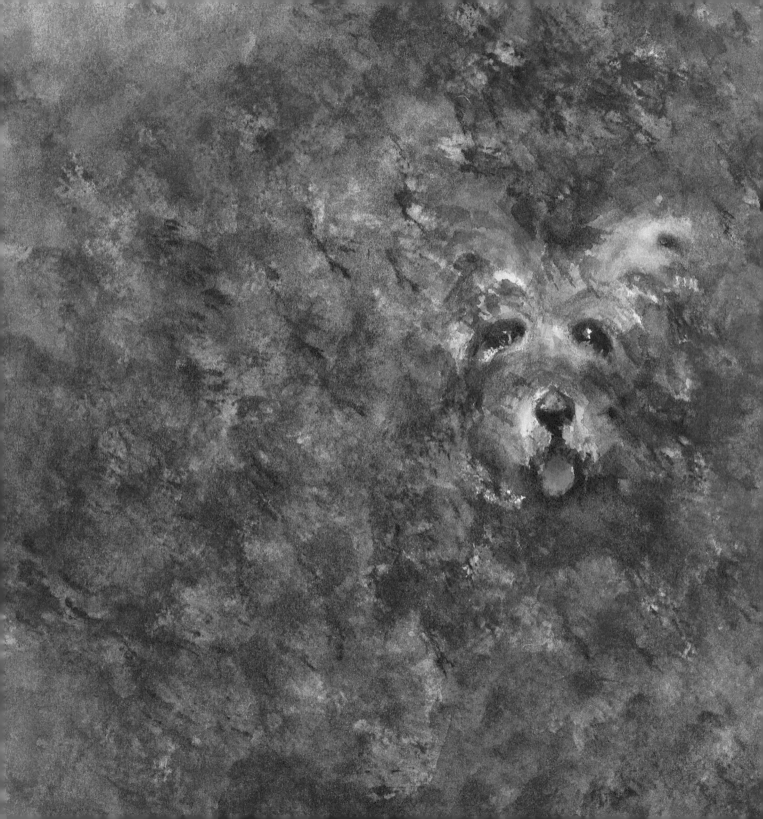

Because so many of the animals
were shy, Mr. Fuzzy Ears thought,

*"I'll just hide and try to catch
whatever little critter passes by."*

But no one came by, and finally
Mr. Fuzzy Ears decided to get help.

Mr. Fuzzy Ears talked to his mom and dad about his search. And they knew exactly where to look.

Of course! They went to the Humane Society!

Mr. Fuzzy Ears said, "I remember this place!
This is where Mom and Dad found me.
They were so good to me and
helped me find my Forever Home!"

The first friend Mr. Fuzzy Ears met was a striped cat named Preston. They sniffed noses and really liked each other, but Preston had just come to the Humane Society and was too sick to find his new home yet.

Preston told Mr. Fuzzy Ears that his human couldn't afford Preston's medical care, so he was brought to the Humane Society.

Mr. Fuzzy Ears didn't worry, though, because he knew Preston would be loved and cared for at the Humane Society and that they would find him just the right home when it was time!

Then Mr. Fuzzy Ears met Rae, a cute little fuzzy rat, swinging in her hammock.

Rae's human had moved to a place that didn't allow animals, so her human brought Rae to the Humane Society.

The good news was that Rae already had a family pick her and was waiting for her forever family to take her home.

This was a very good day!

Mr. Fuzzy Ears spotted a fluffy little
rabbit and asked about her story.
Her name was Scamper.

Someone had given Scamper to a child as
an Easter present. But the child didn't know
how to take care of a rabbit, so Scamper
was brought to the Humane Society.

Scamper hoped she would find a family
who knows that having a pet is an
important responsibility and be
ready to love and take care of her
when it's her time to be adopted.

Then Mr. Fuzzy Ears saw
a sad dog named Izzy.

She was very unhappy, but
when she saw Mr. Fuzzy Ears,
she smiled and said, "Are you
looking for a friend? Please
take me home with you!"

Mr. Fuzzy Ears looked at Mom
and Dad and they said, "Yes!"

Izzy said,

"Thank you!
    But may I also
bring a friend?"

"The little girl dog next to me is Sofie, my best friend,"
said Izzy. "We both came from a place with lots of dogs where
we were all kept in small cages and not allowed to play."

"Sofie is very shy but very sweet. And we would be so happy if
both of us came to live with you. Okay?"

Mom and Dad said, "Yes."
Mr. Fuzzy Ears was delighted!

This was a very,
very good day!

They all jumped into the car and headed
to Mr. Fuzzy Ears' house.

But on the way home,
they saw a small furry creature
trotting along the road.

They stopped the car to see
what it was. It was a very small
puppy who said his name
was Teddy and he was lost.

They put Teddy in the car and took him home
to care for him until they could find his family.

The next day, Mom and Dad put up signs
to try to find Teddy's family.

They called their animal doctor to see if they
knew anyone who had lost a puppy.

They called the Humane Society to see if they
knew of anyone looking for a lost puppy.

But no one seemed to be looking for Teddy.
So Teddy, too, came to live with Mr. Fuzzy Ears' family.

After searching so
long for a furry
friend, Mr. Fuzzy Ears
now had three friends
to play with.

Now, every day is a very good day!

Mr. Fuzzy Ears
and his family

Pictured from left to right:
Izzy, Scamp (Mr. Fuzzy Ears),
Teddy and Sofie, the official dogs
of Bradley University. Also pictured
are the author and her husband.

Like Mr. Fuzzy Ears on Facebook and
follow Mr. Fuzzy Ears on Instagram.

iUniverse books may be ordered through booksellers or by contacting:

iUniverse
1663 Liberty Drive
Bloomington, IN 47403
www.iuniverse.com
1-800-Authors (1-800-288-4677)

Because of the dynamic nature of the Internet, any web addresses or links contained in this book may have changed since publication and may no longer be valid. The views expressed in this work are solely those of the author and do not necessarily reflect the views of the publisher, and the publisher hereby disclaims any responsibility for them.

ISBN: 978-1-5320-6170-7 (sc)
978-1-5320-6172-1 (hc)
978-1-5320-6171-4 (e)

Library of Congress Control Number: 2018913057

Print information available on the last page.

iUniverse rev. date: 10/29/2018

CPSIA information can be obtained
at www.ICGtesting.com
Printed in the USA
LVHW072017040119
602831LV00001B/1/P